AF822624

Military March in D Major

PRIMO

Franz Schubert (1797-1828)
Op. 51, No. 1; D. 733

* *Fingerings and material in parentheses are editorial. Although Schubert left no pedal indications, short amounts of pedal may be used at the discretion of the players. The editor recommends pedaling be done by the secondo player.*

This edition is dedicated to Arlene Krueger and Solveig Steen, with appreciation and admiration.
—*Maurice Hinson*

SECONDO

PRIMO

* *Play the notated short appoggiaturas (♪ and 𝅘𝅥𝅯) in measures 29–31, 35, 39, 42, 81 and 85 as acciaccaturas (♪), sounded simultaneously with the following note.*

Fine

44
p
fp
50
cresc.
f
56
1.
fz
fz
62
2.
8
ff
fz
Fine

Trio

PRIMO

87
p
93
99
p
105
Marcia D.C. al Fine
cresc.
p
cresc.